WITHDRAWN

The Shoebox

of

Desire

and other tales

ALLEN WOODMAN

Illustrated by Ross Zirkle

Swallow's Tale Press

Additional copies of this book may be had by sending $7.95 (for paperbound) or $13.95 (for cloth) and 50 cents postage to:

Swallow's Tale Press
P. O. Box 930040
Norcross, GA 30093

We thank the following magazines for permission to reprint some of these stories. Please support literary magazines, for they support young writers.

The North American Review
Epoch
Swallow's Tale Magazine
Carolina Quarterly
Akros Review
Crescent Review

ISBN 0-930501-10-1 (cloth)
ISBN 0-930501-11-X (paper)

Library of Congress Catalog Number: 86-63358

Printed in The United States of America. Typesetting and printing by CLS Printing of Tallahassee, Florida.

TABLE OF CONTENTS

The Shoebox

of

Desire

and other tales

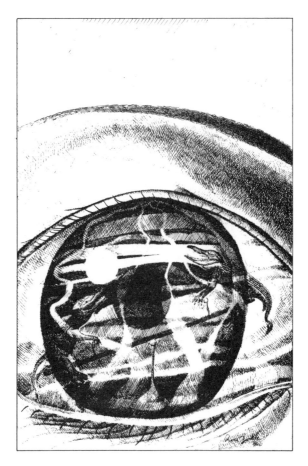

For my parents, Inez and Sandy;
and for Ray Carver and Joy Williams

VINYL REPAIR

VINYL REPAIR

Noble was absently sprinkling salt over half a ripe tomato when he saw something black lying in the sand next to the shoreline. He had been re-coloring the vinyl seats in the High Tide Motel lobby from blue to red, and was now taking a few minutes for lunch. It was off-season and no one was in a hurry.

The black spot turned out to be an abandoned bikini top. Noble examined it. It had a label that read, "Cole of California, Size 36B." It pleased Noble to look at it. He hadn't expected such an item.

Noble thought about the act of a woman in white-hot summer pulling her top off and smoothing her skin with smears of cream or lotion. It was easy for him to love the things of people he didn't know.

Once he had a job repairing the mayor's chair. Some kids had broken into his office and burned holes on the arms of his desk chair with cigarettes. The chair was only brown naugahyde, but it had once belonged to the mayor's father. Noble fixed the arms and re-conditioned the whole chair so well that when the mayor sat down in it and rubbed his hands across the places where the damage had been he started to cry. Noble followed suit in a friendly, unreasoned way. It was like he had loved that old chair, too. Neither of the men was known for easy tears.

Noble held each cup of the top in his palms and imagined the breasts that once filled them. Then he replaced it on the sand where he had found it. Noble walked back to the lobby and started re-coloring the seats. Colleen came out from behind the front desk to watch. He was going to tell her about the bikini top, but he didn't. He thought it'd be like telling a secret someone had made him promise not to tell.

"That red color's good. It's what the lobby needed," Colleen said.

Noble placed his brush into the Perma-Bond Color Coat can. "This'll color anything," he said, and pointed to his white shoes. "Guess how old my shoes are?"

"They look brand new," she said.

"Three years old. I coated them myself a week ago."

Colleen brought out a pair of white shoes from her kitchenette in the back. "Can you make these new again?" she asked.

"Wherever I see vinyl, I can do business," he said, and traced his fingers along the shoes' outlines.

"They were my wedding shoes," Colleen said. "My Warren loved me so much that he tried to kill me with them. He threw me around this very lobby one night. I kept banging into those chair legs. Then he pulled the shoes off my feet and started hitting me on the head with them. He kept shouting parts of the wedding vows, 'To have and to hold. Till death do you part.'"

"What happened?"

"Since then, I've never been able to go to another wedding. I can't even stand to watch one on TV."

"No, I mean about your husband?"

"He shot himself in room seventeen. A guest heard the shot and told me. When I opened the door, I didn't even recognize him. I thought it was some tourist."

Noble waited to speak. He could feel she had more words to get out.

"If the Tastee-Freez hadn't been closed he would still be alive. Everytime we had a fight he'd go next door and have a chocolate malted. Sometimes he'd bring me back a cup of soft-serve. But this time the Tastee-Freez closed early. There was a closed sign on the door. The boy inside cleaning up remembered my husband coming by and banging on the glass."

Noble didn't know what to say. They were just standing there looking at each other, and looking at the shoes.

"I'll restore these free for you. But tell your friends I charged you three dollars," Noble said.

She offered him a cup of coffee. She had just made a fresh

pot.

Noble sat down on the sofa in Colleen's room. The sofa was perfect. No holes or cracks in the vinyl. Colleen gave him some coffee and sat down beside him.

"Doesn't sound much like love," Noble said.

"It was love."

"The way he beat you with your wedding shoes?"

"It was true," Colleen insisted.

Noble lifted his coffee mug in salute. The mug had an illustration of a card from a Monopoly game. It was Boardwalk. Monopoly was Noble's favorite board game as a child. He wondered if his childhood edition was still around, stored in an attic someplace. It was nice to think about that game for a few seconds. He remembered giving it up about the same time he stopped reading the Sunday comics. "Then love is knowing what to overlook," he finally said.

Then he did something. He didn't know what else to do. He picked up her hand. He felt the hard bones under her skin. What good bones, he thought.

Afterwards they sat up on the sofa. Their knees bumped. "Now say something so I don't feel like a whore," Colleen said.

Noble took her hand again and raised it to his lips. He was thinking about the tan lines that made cuts where her torso had been separated from the sun. She looked like some sort of board for a game that had not been created yet. The sections of unsunned flesh seemed luminous.

"We are all so lucky," he said, and thought about how the vinyl coating he would use on her shoes would be sturdy and how it would last longer than anything else.

THE CRUELTY OF CHAIRS

THE CRUELTY OF CHAIRS

The chairs waited in the Trout brothers' converted basement workshop. They had waited such a long time that they had forgotten what they had remembered of the forest. They had become horrible. They dreamed of breaking old men's backs.

Harry Trout waited in the basement as well. Harry made the exquisite hand-turned legs and frames, and Dave, his younger brother, fashioned the delicate cane bottoms. Together they erected chairs that were wondrous to behold. But wonderwork was out of fashion, and sales were few.

Harry's face was gentle and distant. He was not thinking about the chairs or the pains of old men's backs, even though he was an old man. What he was doing was dreaming backwards of a woman who lived in another time. He dreamed of caressing Sarah Bernhardt's leg.

It was an article in the "That's Entertainment" section of the local newspaper that had started Harry's reverie. The paper was small enough that a section on amusements and the obituary column were on the same page. The article told how Dr. Denucé amputated Sarah's afflicted right leg, almost to the hip, on February 15, 1915, and how P.T. Barnum offered her ten thousand dollars to display the severed leg in his exhibition. After her convalescence in a pine-surrounded villa overlooking the tranquil Bay of Arcachon, the doctor tried to fit her with a wooden leg that was attached by a heavy girdle that clung about her hips and stomach. But Sarah hated the idea of ever wearing any sort of corset. She flew into a rage and ordered the thing thrown into the fire.

Sarah's solution was to have a litter chair specially designed with two horizontal supports by which she could be borne about. It was finished in Louis XV style, painted white and ornamented with gilt carvings. And when she was carried about she assumed the attitude of an empress in a ritual procession. Her arms full of roses. Her wild hair crowned with a capote of flowers. Her mutilated figure a mass of velvets.

Dave, the cane-weaving brother, finished eating a bowl of Raisin Bran and drinking the last beer in the house. He smiled a moment thinking to himself how Harry had earlier picked the raisins out of his own toast so that Dave could have extra fruit with his cereal. Dave wished the telephone would ring. He had gotten bored with reading the "Comics" section that Harry had left for him on the kitchen table. He wanted another beer, but Harry would only let him have one a day. It was not that Dave was a heavy drinker, but he was weak in the head. People had said so often enough for him to hear, and he had to remain clearheaded for the caning.

If the phone rang, he would answer as Harry had taught him to do, "Trout Brothers' Chairs. Chairs the Three Bears would love." Actually, Harry had taught him to say that many years before. Now, Harry would just as soon Dave answered the phone with a simple "Hello" or "Trout Brothers' Chairs."

Ten more minutes passed as Dave waited for the phone to ring. He picked the receiver up, stared at it, and practiced answering. The telephone was the silent black kind.

Dave climbed down the steps into the basement and stood by Harry.

Harry's eyes were closed. His mouth moved like he was eating a chocolate bar. Then his eyes opened slowly to see Dave staring at him. "Did you like your cereal?" Harry asked.

Dave nodded his head. "Yes, Harry. What you been doing down here?" Dave didn't want to tell Harry that every time he found him asleep, he was afraid that Harry was really dead, gone, and had left him behind.

Harry read Dave the article about Sarah Bernhardt's leg.

"How awful," Dave cried. "So what did she end up doing with her leg?"

"I don't know," Harry answered. "She probably had it

cremated with the wooden one."

"Sarah Bernhardt," Dave said, letting the name float in the air with nothing to follow, as if he were repeating a name someone had given him over the phone.

Later that afternoon, the Trout brothers got into their Ford pickup and drove in silence to visit Otto at the home.

Otto Maddox was a war buddy of Harry's. Otto had even been decorated for heroism. But when Otto returned from the war and found out that his wife had made a career move from beautician to poodle groomer, well, Otto gritted his teeth. Fighting overseas so his wife could blue-tint a retired housewife's hair seemed ethical enough, but the very thought that he had killed so that his wife could paint poodle toenails changed Otto.

"Jeez," was all he said. Then he picked up one of the client's toy poodles by the hind legs, held it carefully away from him, and swung the dog like a baseball bat. The dog's head kept connecting with his wife's head. Their yelping merged. The dog was small, but tough, and so was the wife.

Flora, his wife, and Sassha, the poodle, weren't injured but the pet's owner never returned Sassha to Flora's. Flora had photographs made showing the bruises on her neck and shoulders. She had Otto placed in a special home.

The home had a colonial facade with a row of rocking chairs chained to the porch. Dave rubbed his hand over the seat of one of the rockers. He wondered if the owners of the home thought they needed the chains to keep the chairs from sneaking away in the night. "This is where Otto lives," Dave said to nobody.

The Trout brothers were surprised that Otto was not in his room. The windows were wide open. A cleaning woman was going over the room. The TV set that was usually playing *Hogan's Heroes* about this time was dead quiet.

For a moment Harry thought they had entered the wrong room. The floor was wet. Everything smelled of Lysol and soap. Then he noticed the medal-clad uniforms still hanging in the wardrobe.

The cleaning woman straightened up. "He's been moved to the freight room. They need this room for a new patient. It's a shame he died. He was the only war hero we ever had, but I can't for the life of me remember which war he was in."

Harry sent Dave to wait out front. Then he stopped in the restroom to wipe his face with some cool water. In the mirror, he saw the reflected row of black-seated toilets and the dried bits of excrement beside every commode. There was no need to curse the old people. They were weak and taking strong medicine. It happened before they could sit down.

Harry tried to open the door to the freight room. It was locked. He felt like kicking it in, but he knew his foot couldn't budge the steel deadbolt.

He found the cleaning woman in the auditorium. She was tearing down and storing two-hundred white chairs. The white chairs wanted to stay put. They wanted to be covered with dust. Harry helped her with them. He even started humming, thinking about the patients two-stepping on the cleared floor that night. And he imagined Sarah Bernhardt's leg in the center of them all, hopping and kicking and dancing unencumbered.

Outside, Dave thought Harry was going to say something, but he didn't. Dave knew what had happened.

Harry sat down in one of the plain rockers beside Dave. He started to rock, but the chain kept holding the chair back. Dave looked at Harry's eyes.

Dave reached over and squeezed his brother's hand for a minute. When he let go of it, he felt strange, like somehow he was suddenly made Harry's older brother.

Dave looked at the rocking chair he was sitting in. He wondered how it would look painted white and ornamented in gilt carvings. He patted its armrest. He motioned for Harry to get in the truck. In his mind he was already breaking the chains.

GULF

GULF

Martha lived alone in a trailer in Destin, Florida, on Highway 98. She was thirty-one. She would sit in the trailer watching wrestling matches on TV all night and work at the pier selling frozen shrimp for bait all day. Martha was afraid she would try to do her laundry at the post office or mail her letters to her father in the washing machine.

"People have a limited capacity for tragedy," Martha told Ceil, her neighbor. "Mine is limited like the number of shrimp you get on a seafood platter."

Ceil sat up in an E-Z Go golf cart in front of her trailer with the dignity of one of those ladies who sit up all night in airports waiting on mythical flights. The golf cart sat up on concrete blocks. "When you live alone you see little things add up in big damages."

"It's so silly," Martha continued. "I think how meaningless everything has become except for two or three things."

The pier was a distraction. For seventy-five cents a day, tourist daddies would leave their children to fish with Snoopy rods and reels, haul in croakers and bash their fishness and brains on the warm, dark planks until they returned from drinking draft beer to unhook them. Throughout the distance of the pier and the heat, Martha could hear it, the gurgled croaking of the fish and the bamm bamm bamm.

There was not much to do in Destin. People walked, fished and swam in the surf. Most people stayed for short periods of time. But there were the old women who seemed to have always been there. Martha watched them on the beach searching for sand dollars. They were happy women wearing large straw hats and the whitest clothes Martha had ever seen.

The old women made the largest sand dollars into clocks and

painted the faces in bright acrylic flowers. The perfect, smaller ones they framed on red velvet above a card that told of the legend of the sand dollar.

On Martha's day off, she would follow them up the beach. She would imagine that the old women were giant sea birds picking the shoreline clean. They discarded the tiny, broken sand dollars. Sometimes Martha would pick up the rejected ones and carefully place them into the cups of her bikini top against her small breasts and let the salt water wash them out.

On Martha's birthday, she called her father. "I like to be alone at night and water my lawn," her father's voice said.

Martha turned on the TV. It was time for *The Andy Griffith Show*. Andy and Barney were looking through a box full of stuff from their old high school days. And Barney came up with a rock, and looked at it a long time in silence and said, "You know what this is?" And Andy said, "What?" "My dad's rock," Barney said. And they both looked at that dumb rock, and then Barney explained that his dad used to strike matches on it when he was a little boy, and he would watch him.

Martha asked Ceil about things.

"Discipline is what it takes," Ceil said. "I had a small insurance policy on my Horace when he totalled the Cadillac. I booked a tour of Europe, a series of teas and playgoing. I wasn't impressed. The passion plays were boring. All that stood out to me was Venice, Italy. The thing that excited me the most was something I found in the back of one of those world famous boutiques."

Ceil left her post in the golf cart, took Martha inside her trailer and handed her a small glass object. Inside, two green alligators were on a seesaw. There was a beach scene in the background with a sun Martha couldn't tell was rising or setting.

Ceil shook Martha's hand that held the paperweight so that a snowstorm began. White flakes fell slowly making the seesaw go up and down. *Florida* was inscribed on it. "At first I thought it was just a funny souvenir to find in a Venice gift shop. Then it struck me that it was some kind of a sign. When I returned, I sold my house and its memories and moved straight down the highway to Florida. Now I pass my time placing bets on which side of the seesaw will finish on top."

Martha wondered why Ceil's trailer always smelled like chili and fried fish.

Ceil pointed to some shelves and Martha could see hundreds of neatly stacked glass paperweights. "That's what I mean by discipline," Ceil said.

Martha and Ceil walked to the beach. They stood in the sand with the water up to their necks, so that their bobbing heads looked like fishermen's floats.

"My father used to bring me to the beach and blow the ocarina until morning," Martha said.

"What's an ocarina?"

"It resembles something like a sweet potato." Martha pretended to hold one and mouthed three shrill toots. "My father and I'd talk between numbers. I remember walking with him and pointing out floating condoms. He'd say they were balloons from party boats. For a long time after that I imagined a fabulous Gulf of Mexico brimming over with ships decorated with crepe paper flags and balloons. I even asked my father if I could have my next birthday party on one of the boats."

"My father was just the opposite," Ceil said. "There was the time in New York at the Thanksgiving Day Parade. A 60-foot-long balloon moose passed over our heads, wagging in the breeze, lurching ever closer to the street. It took thirty people to handle it. They wore green ribbons that read, Inflation Team.

"The next morning, my father took me down to 36th and 7th to watch them take Bullwinkle apart. All the balloons I ever deflated had simply rocketed violently off, emitting sounds you wouldn't want to make in church, but the workmen slowly wound the ropes connecting the balloon down on sticks — an antler, a leg at a time. Bullwinkle slowly lost his moosey features."

Martha started playing one of those tunes that somehow sounds like it ought to be familiar yet isn't on her imaginary ocarina; Ceil cupped her hands and pretended to play an ocarina, too. Then they both just leaned back into the water, feeling like balloons whose mooring lines are being cast off one by one.

TV GUIDE

TV GUIDE

Ray took our TV.

He came home after work and caught me watching it alone. That was not the deal. I could watch it when he was with me. He thought I was obsessed. He thought the bald man on the TV-rental commercial was giving me special coded messages of love over the airwaves.

I woke up late the next morning. In place of the TV sat a large green bird in a cage. The thought of it terrified me. Ray knew what would bring me the most pain.

I paced the floor like a trapped animal, waiting for Ray to return home. I did not go near the birdcage. I expected some kind of explanation. There was none.

Ray ate his mansize, beefsteak TV dinner. His greasy lips did not speak a word.

That night I dreamed Ray and I were listening to one of those answer-man type radio programs and eating fried chicken. Ray thought I should listen more to the radio and less to TV. He tried to make a joke saying that it would make me less stationary. A woman caller was speaking on the radio. She said, "I only feel alive when I'm eating sunflower seeds in front of the pigeons at the park." There was static. The host of the radio show was explaining how you had to turn your radio off or at least down in volume before calling in your question. Ray was eating a chicken wing that didn't look very well done. He gave out with a choking laugh. Then he fell face down in to the Barrel-O-Chicken and died right there. The next thing in the dream, I'm at the grocery store buying a cart full of frozen chicken parts. I mean, I've got this passion for them.

I awoke to what sounded like Ray having an orgasm. It was not a loud thing, just a little sound like someone saying one of the vowels with the exception of Y. I felt around on top of me; he wasn't there. All was quiet, except for a peculiar scratching sound.

I descended the stairs. A light shone from the den. I knew I never left a light on. I peeked around the corner of the doorway in order to see something.

It was Ray. He was trying to teach the bird to talk. He had my copy of *The World's Best Loved Quotations*. Ray had given it to me to help me utilize my time better. He was reading through it to see which one the bird might like. "'Between grief and nothing I will take grief,'" he said softly to the bird. "That's Faulkner, a novelist." His fingers grazed the bars of the cage. I was pained to see how familiar they were.

The next morning Ray went to work without breakfast, without repeating his old joke about how Corn Chex was the national cereal of Czechoslovakia, and I just sat and listened to the water drip through the Mr. Coffee filter.

I decided to take the bird back to the pet shop where Ray had purchased it. I found the receipt in his sock drawer.

It was a small store called Fins, Furs, and Feathers. The cages were stuck among the rubber bones and doggie shampoos. A sign above the cages read, The Ideal Pet.

The saleswoman seemed too large for the store. She said she always loved birds. In her hand she held a napping bird. It looked dead.

As she returned the cage back among the others, she asked me if she looked eighty-seven years old. I said she didn't. It was the truth. She had these real good bones, the kind you know are hard just by looking at them.

"The secret to youth," she said, "is transcending the physical, ESP." She looked at the birdcages. All the birds seemed to come to life with song. It sounded like music you wanted to hear inside only and nowhere else.

I thought about how that kind of communication could change my life.

With the refund, I bought another TV. It wasn't near as nice as the original set. It had initials carved in the simulated wood frame. It didn't have remote control. But I didn't want to waste time shopping around.

Ray got home late that night.

I was in the kitchen making ham sandwiches. It's what I usually did whenever there was trouble. After wrapping all the sandwiches in plastic wrap, I put them in the freezer. Ray would have lunch made for weeks, I thought.

Ray entered the kitchen.

I was just sitting at the table, feeling for dead skin on my scalp, and waiting for the automatic dishwasher to shut off so I could check the stainless for spots.

"What would you have me do if you had your way?" he asked. I said nothing. I stared at him with the silence of animals. I wanted to be restored by the silence, to restore Ray, to restore our home.

Ray put his hand on my knee. "We have to have a little realism around here," he said.

Something about that word *realism* smacked me like a board across the heart.

The hand stroking my knee seemed larger than I'd ever realized.

It was ten o'clock. It was time for the newscast. I opened us both a beer. On the TV something important was being said. I turned off the sound. Ray and I stretched out on the couch. For a moment, I thought about the things that might have spilled between the cushions over the years: pencils, coins, matches, combs.

Ray patted my hair. The couch was warm. The vinyl stuck to my skin. Ray's movements blurred in the grey light of the TV. His face became a cloudy image. I clung hard to him. I tried to kiss him.

"What's wrong?" he asked.

"I love you, too," I said.

FATHERS

FATHERS

At one time he worked in a small, sad barber shop all alone. It was not far from where my mother and I lived. When I needed a haircut, she would send me to him.

The only things personal about the shop were an old circus poster and his smell, which remained on his barber's smock after he was dead and made me cry as much as the knowledge that I would soon forget him.

My father would place his hands on both sides of my head as if he was making a tiny frame for my face. He wouldn't say anything. Barbering took him past speech. He would just look in the mirror at me. And I would look in the mirror at him, too. I would notice the way the mock crewneck collar of his smock made him look like a priest. He would run his fingers through my hair like a thick comb, still staring in the mirror at me, but he would never tell me what he saw.

There was nothing to do with me after the haircut, except to go over to the Kottage Restaurant for their vegetables. They were fresh, and you could get three with any dinner. My father said he brought my mother there once, but they gave her an eating utensil that wasn't too clean.

Amidst the sprinkles of sugar crystals on the tablecloth and the salt and pepper shakers that didn't match, my father would tell me his father's story. "My father," he would say, "was a great man. Short and bald, but still a champion gymnast. They would launch him out of the circus cannon with a puff of smoke 60 feet through the air, and always he was caught safely. From the net he would leap to his feet to stand for the ovation of the crowd.

"How he did it not even I knew. Maybe it was a giant coiled spring and a huge firecracker? My mother wouldn't let him show me how. She wanted me to have a real career." My father stirred his coffee; the teaspoon sounded like a bell clapper. He smiled at his own foolishness.

"Once he let me climb atop his cannon," my father continued, gesturing with the pepper shaker. "But he never ever let me slip down the barrel."

We would walk to the cashier and wait for the waitress to come forward to tell the cashier what we had bought. The waitress wore a black shiny apron over a dingy white nylon dress. I wouldn't look at her, but I knew what she looked like anyway.

Then my father would say, "Better finish trimming your hair. Can't let you leave with your hair shaped like a Christmas tree." He would take me back and sit me in his chair. He would clip the ends of a few hairs with scissors, simply to keep me from leaving him. And I would look at the circus poster and think about his father, and how my father's story of his father was like having a familiar music box that didn't have to be opened for you to hear the music.

Finally, before I had to go, he would take a bottle of hard candy out of a half empty drawer and offer me some. It was sad, the taste of the candy and the way the candy stuck together.

ALICE AND ALLIE

THE SHOEBOX OF DESIRE

Alice and I ate dinner in her kitchen. After coffee, she pulled out her shoebox of real life stories of fertility and desire. She cut them out of newspapers and magazines. She saved them until someone visited, then she read them aloud.

Alice scratched the polish off her nails while she spoke.

The first clipping was about a woman who had crabs, but didn't know. She thought she had caught fleas from her cat. She tried dusting herself with flea powder. Then an article appeared in a leading woman's magazine that explained about the crab epidemic.

The woman was dating a married man. She hoped to give them to him, to give to his wife. She hoped this would make the wife leave him. She wanted to marry the man. It never happened.

Another story was about a phobia in China called *shook-yong*. A man believed that his penis would disappear into his abdomen and that he would die. To prevent this, he gripped his penis firmly. When he grew tired, his wife, friends, and relatives lent a hand. A specialist constructed a wooden clasp and recommended his wife apply fellatio immediately. The victim's spirits were lifted.

Many other young men have since been accused of feigning *shook-yong*.

The final story was about a man who won a free dinner for two. He won it on a flight from Atlanta for having the oldest penny on the plane. He didn't think he had a chance to win. The penny was dated 1964.

The man did not know anyone in San Francisco to eat with.

On the way to his motel the man thought he saw some cobalt blue Depression era glass at a yard sale. He got out of his rental car and examined things. He lit a cigarette. He picked up a pigeon-blood vase.

The house looked empty.

A woman came down the sidewalk carrying a grocery bag. She had tremendous thighs.

"Hello," she said to the man.

"I thought no one was here," he said.

"It's a pretty good vase," she said and put down the bag. "How much?"

"Make me an offer," she said and pulled out two cans of beer. She offered the man one.

"Is it a copy?" he asked.

"A copy?" She laughed. "Two things I grabbed when my dad threw me out and chased me down the street, that vase and a big box of Kotex."

"He threw you out?"

"I drank a little wine. Kept it in that vase. Nothing wrong in that, but I was scared of my dad. I feared him. He seldom put his hand on me, but his look, just his look, was enough to tell me I had better keep quiet and take what was coming to me. A lot of times I'd just as soon he slapped me in the face than look at me that way."

The woman also told the man that as a child she had been so beautiful that she had once been mistaken for a princess. She said that she had been such a young bride that she played with dolls. And she told once again how her dad had chased her down the street with her carrying the vase and the sanitary napkins, only this time she mentioned another man and a shotgun.

The man told the woman about the free dinner tickets. He asked if she would like him to pick her up later in the rented car.

I thanked Alice for the food and stories. She asked me what I thought they all meant. I said that maybe desire isn't conditional. She agreed, but I'm not sure she understood. I'm not sure I understood.

We decided to have more coffee.

LIFE STORY

Alice was trying to tell her life story at the same pace at which a dying man's life is said to pass in review before his eyes.

"My father," she said, " caught a mouse one day, tied a little string around his neck, and I walked it up and down the street.

"I took it by my grandmother's. She lived in a red-brick house. It had tall chimneys and a garden of blood-colored roses. I don't remember much about her except her size. I liked to watch and see if she'd be able to rise from her chair.

"In my grandmother's dining-room there was a glass-fronted cabinet and in the cabinet a few black feathers and the skeleton of a bird.

"I asked my grandmother what they were used for. She said it was what was left of the blackbird that killed my grandfather.

"My grandmother told me how the blackbird had flown through my grandfather's office window, busting the glass and killing itself. The blackbird's fatal course cut off the top of its skull. It flopped in shards of glass on his desk, frantically beating broken wings. It trembled and died.

"Grandfather took sick at once. A janitor was called to sweep up the debris. Grandfather went home.

"Grandfather's voice grew faint as a soft wind. In his mind the bird's death was a curse. He put the blame on a woman who wanted to get on a bus he once drove for a previous job.

"The woman tried to take a chicken and a goat on the bus with her. 'Sorry, no goats,' my grandfather told her. 'Since when no goats?' she asked. 'I never let goats ride,' he said. 'What about the chicken?' 'Chickens are O.K.'

"The woman handed the goat's lead rope to a waiting child. The chicken flew from the woman's arm into the bus, defecating all the way to the back. 'One more question,' the woman began, but before she could gather her breath to utter it, Grandfather said the answer to all questions that shouldn't be asked, 'To get to the other side.'

"There was sharp silence for a moment, then a ripple of delayed laughter struck the passengers on the bus. The woman did not laugh with them, but let out a short scream like that of squeaky bed wheels being moved or someone weeping and dying. Then she ran away in the direction the child had taken the goat.

"After that Grandfather acted strange. He would no longer drive the bus. He thought the thorns on the roses looked like bird beaks. He took a desk job in a tall office building.

"I liked to stick what was left of the feathers into the skeleton to try and make the bird look real. I always pestered Grandmother for them. I never wanted anything as much as I wanted those feathers and bones.

"When Grandmother died, I thought, 'Now I can have the blackbird.' But my father said, 'Oh, those old feathers and bones. I'm afraid I threw them away.'

"I left school after the eighth grade. I worked for a while in a hospital. I emptied the patients' purses and took their urine samples to the lab.

"There was one woman's urine that looked thick as pudding. You could have cut it with a knife.

"This was the funniest part of my life. The place was a snake pit. They had one room for women. It was a big circle of beds.

"There was one woman there who said they locked her up because she couldn't find her mouth to eat with. She threw the food on her chest. But everyday she'd still manage to put a little plate on the floor for her dog. When no one was looking, I'd pick the plate up and put it back on the table because I didn't want the doctors to know she was feeding a dog who wasn't there. The dog's name was Sue Sue.

"They brought another woman in. Someone had tried to cut her head off. She was slit from ear to ear. They locked her up in a special room. You could hear her banging her head off all night.

"What else can I tell you, Allie? I wanted to be married. I lived in an apartment with roaches everywhere. I kept a hammer in one hand. I bought fancy underwear. I was a virgin until my first wedding night although I allowed an orderly at the hospital once to put his hand under my whites.

"I thought I was pregnant once. The doctor said 'Four months.' I told him I still had my period."

"I remember seeing two legs going up. I didn't know they were mine. I felt something scraping me. The doctor said, 'It isn't a pregnancy.'

"They held this thing in front of me on forceps. The doctor said it was my twin. It had gotten inside of me in my mother's womb. I wondered whether it would have been my brother or sister.

"Were it not ongoing, that might be a scene to remember. The one that offered the least satisfaction." Alice clicked her tongue, and then lit a cigarette.

I wondered about the point of Alice's story. I reminded myself that she had had two coronaries and three marriages. I guessed that some life stories don't have a point. The most beautiful ones are irrational gifts. And maybe a friend should know less about a friend after hearing her life story, not more.

STILL POINTS

Alice leaned in close and whispered, "You are not astonished enough by your own life." She was grinning. Her face was like a child's equation written on a blackboard.

Her nurse came in and gave her injections. While the nurse was away, Alice made friendly indecent proposals.

I thought about that Mexican girl who had hundreds of needles inside her. The newspaper said she didn't feel any pain until they emerged through the skin. A priest counted two-hundred and thirteen needles coming out of her buttocks, breasts, and insides of her thighs.

"I've decided to make a list of things that astonish me about my life," I said to Alice. The first thing I wrote down was that I watered plants long after they were dead.

Alice asked me to make sure her house shoes were placed in the right direction by her bed so she could step right into them.

"You know Jung's theory of synchronicity?" Alice asked.

"That some things are both familiar and surprising?"

"Like the first time we had sex," Alice said.

"You notice one thing, today, like a lot of dead cats, and you notice the same thing tomorrow." I wondered when the nurse would interrupt us again.

"After you die you probably realize you knew what it was going to be like all along." Alice put part of the chain from her St. Jude medal in her mouth.

I thought about my list again. I tried to note down something about my childhood, but I was not a success as a child.

My art teacher wanted me to draw realistic trees. She told me my green balls with little brown bases didn't look like any trees she'd ever seen. "But I've climbed them, hugged them, and fallen out of them," I said. Still, she gave me a sour look and a note to carry home to my parents.

After that incident I only drew realistic pictures of the sinking of the Titanic. Then the teacher left me alone. The little bow of the ship going down. The darkness. A couple of white lumps on top of the water for the iceberg because ninety-five percent of the iceberg was underwater. And little arms reaching up out of the water.

Alice put her hand on mine. I felt how soft and warm it was, and at the same time I felt the hard bones under her skin. What good bones, I thought.

Alice looked tired. She talked about the death of her children. She worried me, but it was on her mind. She told me of an abortion she had in Atlanta and the Greyhound bus ride home. She described the bus ride in detail, but not the abortion.

The wallpaper in the hospice room was pink. The floor lamp had a great dark pink shade. Old people, men and women, sat on a red sofa in the hall, their canes beside them, or between their legs. They did not talk. They seemed asleep.

Alice handed me a small black and white photograph. The picture was not of a person. It was of a small house. A little square of lawn. A driveway. Bricks and windows. "It's the house I was born in," Alice said. "There used to be a porch out back. My mother and I would sit on it and drink tea and imagine we were at a tea party given by the Mad Hatter in *Alice in Wonderland*. We would ask each other foolish riddles that had no answers and sometimes we would engage in a Lobster Quadrille."

I looked at the photograph again. I longed to see the porch behind the house, but it was just a picture of the front.

"That house is gone now," Alice said. "In fact, all of the houses I've ever lived in are gone."

I understood the worn out feeling that comes with having outlived all of the important structures that framed your life.

Alice asked me how my list was coming. I read her my final entry. It was Eliot, "at the still point of the moving world." I told her how I tended to move towards still points.

"No," she said. "You can't end it that way. That would be a terrible ending."

I blinked to rid my eyes of tears and promised the way a politician does that I would find another ending.

FOREIGN POSTCARD

FOREIGN POSTCARD

Your postcard came today. I don't care to make a great nuisance over what is finished. It does not matter to me now. Once it did. I'll think about it very briefly then forget about it.

The postcard does not show clams waiting in a large bowl on a cutting table. If it did, I could imagine the clams softly opening and closing like the hundreds of secret things we should have revealed.

If that were the postcard, I could imagine you sent it to remind me to go shopping. "Don't forget to buy groceries," you'd say. "Don't forget to eat." But there are no clams giving up their grip on life in the postcard you sent.

What you sent me is a postcard of a train arriving or departing in Ecuador, an anachronism with highly polished Victorian brass, enormous amounts of escaping steam, and extravagantly costumed attendants. It is a first class view with all those cute and lovable ponchoed Indians attractively displayed in the brown landscape. It is a lazy and bastard card that will never increase your wisdom or mine. The inscription reads, "It's a beginning."

It is not the real departure or arrival. The one where hundreds of passengers bleed into the cars, tearing hair, not fitting, and hundreds of others try to get out of the cars, smashing themselves with huge baskets, jabbing steel umbrellas into dandruffed shoulders, and sliding into tunnels of rain-beaded orphans, Indian farmers, and clowns in half make-up.

The postcard doesn't show the train stops where young prostitutes club guinea pigs to death with broom handles, or a kid in a blue hat pushing an empty wheelbarrow over stone pavement dotted with manure, stops to look at you, then into the sun before falling down in a spasm, curled in a slapping, vomiting ball.

The postcard doesn't show what I would do if I was with you. I would take you to a restaurant where all over the tables lie jigsaws of dried food particles split from countless servings before. As if reading an ancient tablet, I would show you the messages of what was eaten in the place during the wet or dry years. It would be a history of good and bad harvests. We would inspect microcosms of rice, beans, cheese, and wine. And I would wonder why you bothered to ask the waiter for a menu.

We would hear the whistle blow. You would board the train. The train would jerk into motion, and a moment later your waving figure would abruptly be yanked around a curve and into the past, leaving me to wonder if you can even get clams in Ecuador.

THE LAMPSHADE VENDOR

THE LAMPSHADE VENDOR

It was typical. The door was open. It was summer. The TV was on.

A white-haired man dressed in a black and frayed tuxedo came to the door selling lampshades. He was a dignified man transformed by the loss of his hands. He picked up a shade with one of his metal claws. "Sell you a new lampshade?"

I didn't like the shade. I had never even given much thought to the lampshades I already had. I wondered how he lost his hands. I tried to make conversation. "A man knocked on the door yesterday selling mops and brooms. Do you know him?"

He put the lampshade back on his cart. "No relation. I sell shades. You want one?"

I've always loved human activities that are on the way out. I asked him how long he had sold lampshades.

"Fifteen years ago, I had a side-show at all the big fairs, a flea circus. But I was hit hard by hygiene and taste."

"I saw a flea circus once, but no one believes me," I said. "I keep it to myself. But I'd swear I remember a tiny flea wedding and a flea riding on a bicycle."

"I had a little table for the stage, and I would only allow a few chairs for the audience. I had a ballet sequence, a tightrope walk, and a wagon train race. The secret was all in the human flea. They are the only ones with the necessary power to tug and push with their back legs. My fleas were incredible. What stamina. They could perform hundreds of shows a day, and continue for weeks. And at the end of my show, I would roll back my sleeve and invite the performers to dine." The man raised his chrome hooks in the air.

"I read that in Mexico, the Church supported flea art," I said. "Nuns made and sold miniature models of the stations of the cross fashioned out of flea corpses and scrap materials. The fleas kept them from having to carve human figures."

"I had a flea," he said in a quiet voice. "I kept it as a pet. It was the only one I let suck the palm of my hand. I fastened it to a chain of gold no longer than your finger. I attached a perfectly-shaped coach of gold to the chain for the flea to pull."

I thought I'd seen everything. But the way he talked about this pet flea and the perfect gold coach got me to thinking. "Yes," I said, my voice rising, "do you think you could tell me about it again?"

He stared at me. "No," he said, cautiously. "It's hard on me to remember."

I tried to think of a proper response. "I understand," I said, finally.

The man rubbed one of his metal claws against the skin under his chin. "Wait a minute," he said. "Get me something to write with."

He picked up one of the plain white lampshades. I placed a pen in his left claw. It was a felt tip pen that I had forgotten to return to the clerk when I wrote a check at the A & P.

He drew the whole flea circus on the shade, the wedding, the tightrope walker, and a flea ballet. He drew scenes we hadn't even talked about. Finally he drew what I knew had to be the flea on the golden chain, for it rested on the palm of a hand. The hand was perfect.

From time to time I tried to explain to people why I bought the lampshade. After awhile, I moved the lamp next to my bed and shut the bedroom door.

TALES OF RUCAR

1. The Bear Tamers
2. The Church of Summer Sausage
3. The Pleasure Garden of the Root Vegetables

THE BEAR TAMERS

It was enough that his father taught dancing bears to massage the muscles of poor people weary from working all day in the fields of Rucar. The elder of the tribe rubbed a pinch of salt on a small loaf of bread and tore it into two pieces. The bear tamer's son and I exchanged portions before eating them. We were married.

Our wedding-night was enlivened by Bruin, his father's favorite. First my new husband bathed me in milk. Then I lay down on the floor to enjoy the bear's somewhat heavy-footed treatment. My husband beat time with his hand-made drum. I intoned the prayer for starting a journey. My muscles tensed. They let go. Then I don't know what I did. But since then I have never been on particularly good terms with my orgasms.

When I was again among the living, my new husband smiled at me. A cigarette hung from his lips like a wolf's fang. The smoke was like the shadow of a pale angel.

About the subject of love, my grandmother said, "A man has a mouse in his trousers."

About the subject of bears, my grandmother said nothing.

I had lived with her in a place called The Street of Spoons. It was called The Street of Spoons because of the principal profession of the community. The people would collect wood in the forest and carve beautiful spoons out of it. Occasionally an eccentric would move into the area and make wooden combs.

In the autumn many of the women would work as farm laborers. The men preferred to stay closer to home. It was while returning from working on the land that I met the bear tamer and his son.

They were toiling along the road dressed in leather coats

studded with brass ornaments, dragging after them a big black bear. The men's tawny skin and faces were framed in locks of hair that fell like bluish-black snakes upon their necks.

It pleased the men to show off their bear to us. They put on heavenly smiles, disclosing their white teeth.

The older man started imitating castanets by cracking the joints of his fingers. He motioned for the younger to begin banging a drum. Then the older man threw his cap in the air and started strutting about like a peacock.

The bear did not pay much attention to the men beyond giving a low grunt.

The older man began to shout excitedly at it. He kicked its legs apart.

The bear rose up on its hind legs. It danced heavily. It was the sad dance of a tired bear on a hot, dusty road. But we applauded.

The men followed us back to The Street of Spoons to camp for the night.

The houses on The Street of Spoons were made of tree trunks joined by pieces of packing cases. They were only used in the winter-time or when there was rain. Most of the time we slept outdoors on skins.

That night my grandmother served the men Tuica with manaliga. The prune liqueur added a festive touch to the dry maize porridge. With a string, Grandmother cut the bear a large slice and even added some stewed fruit.

After our meal, my husband-to-be told me how they trained the bears. "We heat an iron tray," he said. "And when it is very hot, we set the bear upon it. We play music and beat a drum. The bear feels the heat and begins to hop. After a while, the bear learns to hop just to the rhythms of the drum."

Then he told me how they caught the bears in the mountains.

There were three things I had to do after my new husband and I lay down on the floor together.

One was to carry a lump of sugar under my armpit to ensure the sweetness of my wedding.

Second was to save the pieces of a plate that my husband

broke behind me.

And the third, the most important thing of all, consecrated our carnal union.

My grandmother appeared at the door with a chicken in a sack. I thanked her and told her it would not be needed.

I danced on a table wearing a blood-stained garment. It was the proof my husband's family needed. It was a slow dance. I was tired and sore. All roared with laughter. The wine had gone to their heads.

I climbed down from the table and sat in one of the chairs that surrounded the revelers. The chair legs sank down into the ground. My new husband was drinking with the men and dancing as though possessed. It was like death.

Later someone suggested that the party move on to another house. Three fiddlers led the procession. Some of them carried torches.

I stayed behind with a man and a woman who were quarreling. He told her how he had cut his first wife's nose off for committing adultery. She said that that had seemed fair, but having her banished from the community seemed too harsh.

I heard the bears in the dark scratching paws and legs in an attempt to break their leashes. Or maybe, I thought, they were just practicing their daily leapings and slidings that took them nowhere.

I decided to make the bears more manaliga and stewed fruit, to learn all of their secret names.

About the subject of love, my grandmother said, "A woman marries her lips together."

THE CHURCH OF SUMMER SAUSAGE

The man with big hands, the man whose fingers traced every precious inch of the textured sausages, knew that there were no sausages lovelier or more delicate in form than Anna's.

The man was barely breathing. On St. Ramfir's Day, the choice of sausage carried weight. It was the memory of last year's sausage, the peasants said, that helped put that old foot in front of that other old foot until the holy day arrived again.

Anna was haggling over the price of a chicken with an old woman who sold golden-brown rolls at the next booth. The rolls were sprinkled with honey and walnut. The old woman's breath smelled of breakfast toast.

Anna had brought a half dozen hens to market bound round her neck on a chain. When a bird was purchased, it was torn off the chain and given to the buyer. The remaining chicken heads formed a perfect inventory.

The chickens were only a sideline today. Normally, the market was filled with vegetables and fruit, which became less and less appetizing under the humid heat. What began in the luxuriance of red paprika and the masses of tomatoes piled in heaps beside the cartloads of watermelons ended in the somber stench of decay.

Anna turned to the man in front of her booth. She had sausages to sell before the procession of St. Ramfir's jawbone. "Something?" Anna asked.

"Who can bear these beautiful forms?" the man said. He exposed a set of teeth that could have invented love.

"Beauty looks for its own match," Anna said, admiring the splendidly embroidered cloak of the large man. He was a csikos, a guardian of the horses for a wealthy family.

Anna felt an insect pricking her, and would have lifted up her red muslin skirt to scratch her groin, but she wanted to keep the illusion of a mystery that didn't exist.

Anna's family numbered eight, and all slept on skins and straw on the ground in the same one room hovel. Anna had her own corner and near her slept her sister and her brother-in-law. The ground was hard and the skins smelled. The insects in the skins would wait until the silent watches of the night, until all lay motionless. Then they would inflict their bites.

After Anna scratched fiercely, they would lead her to believe that she had destroyed them. For a moment she would feel free and her body would tingle gratefully. But then the stinging would begin again on her breasts or some different part of her body. Other times the irritation would take the form of a hand moving over her body. It was no sluggish hand, for it travelled straight towards her ragged undergarments. These beasts briefly succumbed to the scratches of her nails, too.

Anna thought about the wishbones in all the hens about her neck. She desired the skill to crack them in the right way. "Bacon makes bold," she said to the man as he selected a sausage.

He stared at her face and noticed how her thick eyebrows seemed to form an uninterrupted straight line. It was the only distinct feature above her slender upper torso. Then his gaze came to rest upon her rather full hips.

Anna seemed to divine his thoughts.

They were interrupted by the sound of church bells that marked the beginning of the procession. A flight of doves was loosed. A band played. And a long line of priests and monks marched through the center of the market followed by nuns veiled in black. Then a woman passed alone in front of the band, walking slowly and proudly. Her black dress was ornamented in gold lace. In her hands she carried the sculpted gold monstrance that contained the jawbone of St. Ramfir.

As the jawbone passed, the men and women in the crowd took bites of sausage and handed pieces of sausages to their children. It was a gesture in honor of the man who gave them their church.

Anna loved to hear her father tell the story of how once in Rucar there lived a rich man who built a beautiful church of stone. The church was his pride, and neither the peasants of the village nor his wife was allowed to enter it. This made everyone angry and his wife stopped cooking for him.

The spiritual head of the village, then, was an old man named Ramfir who worked in the fields everyday beside the other peasants. His heart was heavy with the thought that the people could not worship in the church. So, he talked the peasants into building their own church out of summer sausage right next to the church of stone.

At first the rich man would strut in front of the church of summer sausage. He would ask the peasants if they had ever seen a real church. But then a breeze would blow and bring to the rich man's nose the delicious scent of sausage, even more delicious since his wife had stopped preparing his meals.

At last the day came when the rich man had not enough strength to resist the temptation. He agreed to exchange with the peasants. As soon as he took possession of the appetizing church, he started straight-away to nibble. The first week he ate the door. The second week he could not resist eating the pulpit. And in short time there was nothing left.

Because of St. Ramfir, the poor villagers who could hardly call their souls their own in those days were able to get a fine stone church to pray in.

As the jawbone of St. Ramfir passed Anna's booth, she held a tiny sausage tight and bit into it, tasting the organs together: the liver, the kidneys, and the red slippery heart.

The man waved the remains of his broken sausage. They were both silent. It was the silence that grew out of exact revelations. "Sweet as the showers of summer," he finally said.

Anna slipped her fingers around the chain that encircled her neck. She pulled the ring of hens over her head, but her straight black hair knotted in one link.

His large hands untangled the fine strands, then touched her lips.

The prickly movement under her skin was not like that caused by the insects.

His mustache stole, hair by hair, into her sight.

She was now all the texture that she wore. And he was the one she had anticipated. Beauty looked for its own match.

And suddenly the delicious scent of the summer sausage blurred her breath.

THE PLEASURE GARDEN
OF THE ROOT VEGETABLES

Vula's body no longer resembled the back of a breakfast chair.

Vula's father was glad. He twirled the silver ring on his little finger the way the strangers at the horse fair had twirled their huge mustachios.

Vula's mother brushed Vula's hair. Her hair was flying like a black waterfall.

At the fair, Vula's father had taken her to see the sword swallower. The thick sword slid down the old man's throat. It reminded Vula of the method tiny boys had for swallowing green lizards. The sword disappeared silently. It was the silence Vula's mother had warned her against.

The strange men at the fair had held Vula like a handsome piece of furniture. Her tears formed a curtain of beads over the door they had opened.

Vula's mother had stopped brushing Vula's hair.

Vula's father piled the silver coins on the table in front of her mother. The clinking sound was their only dialogue.

Vula's mother was a large woman. Her body had been toughened by having worked for years in the fields of root vegetables. Today, Vula's mother felt like a sad plant: no leaves, no vine, no flowers. A plant whose one fruit had become too hard to eat.

Vula's mother looked at her small husband. The men of Rucar did not need large frames for the work they did. Her eyes stared at him like the empty shells of mollusks found in upturned soil.

Vula's father understood the look her mother gave him. It was

time to go to the Pleasure Garden of the Root Vegetables.

In Rucar, one thing is never done. No Rucarian will strike or injure a man below the waist. The seed of man is considered too precious to risk. As St. Ramfir wrote in *The Book of Feathers*, "A man's spear of destiny glows like the sacramental chalice and a woman's breasts are scripture." St. Ramfir had worked many years beside the peasants in the fields of Rucar and understood the desire that jangled softly in front of their bellies.

The Book of Feathers is a small book. Church history has it that St. Ramfir was walking in a field of potatoes when above him he saw a white crow. The white crow was soon attacked by a flock of ordinary crows. It fell at St. Ramfir's feet. With the bones and feathers of this crow, St. Ramfir covered what was later to be called *The Book of Feathers.* It is the book that contains all of the Rucarian rules for spiritual fighting.

St. Ramfir's vision in the field was of the Pleasure Garden of the Root Vegetables. It would be the only place in Rucar where violence would be acceptable. The Pleasure Garden would be an open field surrounded by 27 tables, each of which would be covered with food and drink. And, in the very center of the field, there would be one table covered only with root vegetables and the bones of crows and other birds.

Early church history held that the table in the center of the Pleasure Garden represented the white crow and that the 27 tables surrounding the field stood for the number of ordinary crows in the attacking flock. Other people thought that 27 was just a number St. Ramfir enjoyed counting up to.

Vula and her family entered the Pleasure Garden of the Root Vegetables. The rest of the tribe had followed them to the field. The followers busied themselves by filling up the 27 tables with black bread, ham, cutlets, peppers, gherkins, and bottles of Tuica.

Vula's father and mother moved to the center table. Each stood on separate sides of the pile of bones and vegetables. Vula stood by her mother.

The tribe lit the 27 lamps surrounding the Pleasure Garden. The hiss of the blue flames cursed the darkening sky.

Vula's mother clinched a potato so tightly in her fist that when she released it from her grip it was crushed into a mash. She worked herself into a naked passion and then suddenly fired a potato at her husband's minuscule form.

In moments of trial like this it was proper for the rest of the tribe to maintain a fierce and dogged silence. But many of the women in the tribe could feel a secret, silent language scratching in their throats.

Vula's father picked up the bones of a small bird and hurled them back towards Vula's mother. It was a desperate sight to see the mere skeletons of birds flying through the air without the aid of wing or feather.

Bones and vegetables, illuminated by the blue flames, flashed across the table like the ghostly shadows of past meals.

Their throws began to take on fancier flourishes and more structural accuracy; it was as if the very food itself was taking out its own revenge for being pulled from the earth or plucked from the sky.

Finally, Vula took up a firm potato in the palm of her hand. She launched it straight into her father's eye. He crumpled to the ground. Things came to a halt.

Vula and her mother lifted him back onto his feet. The potato had been a small, innocent thing that had reminded Vula's father of the pain that comes to everyone in different forms. The pain in his eye moved him past speech.

He embraced his daughter and wife. He led them to one of the 27 tables and served them generous portions of meat, and poured their drink, and buttered their bread on both sides, and, in this way, asked their forgiveness.

Then the tribe became ferocious over the unexpected beauty found in the way Vula and her mother chewed the food served to them. And they all came before the substantial tables. And they all drank and ate so well that in the morning only the gleaming bones of birds and a few potatoes were left to replenish the table at the center of the Pleasure Garden of the Root Vegetables.

WAITING FOR THE
BROKEN HORSE

WAITING FOR THE BROKEN HORSE

There always remained the doing of things.

Nathan put on his hat. It was an unfashionable felt hat that occasionally he chose to wear. "I'm going out for coffee," he said to Ann, his wife. "Do you have the keys?"

Ann held her face away from his. She was looking at a slick circular that advertised magazines at 50% off and touted a chance to win a vacation home at the beach. They had already retired to a vacation home at the beach.

She decided to subscribe to a magazine called *Farm Wife News*, even though she had never lived on a farm, even though she couldn't think of any future different from her past.

Nathan waited for the silence to break. Silence was part of their relationship.

Nathan dug around again in his pockets. He found the keys. "I've got them," he said.

Once he caught her in an unguarded moment. She was looking in the bathroom mirror. Her mouth was making an occasion out of it. Her lips were the color of ripe red peppers. The color was important to him because he was always afraid of going blind. She was practicing an exercise she had read about in one of her magazines. Her mouth was exaggerating the shape of vowels. It was a positive act, attempting to postpone the haggard skin of long years.

And for a moment he wished that he could place his head down next to hers and mime the gestures that her face was making. And, as if by magic, their faces would laugh together in a kind of toast to the way things can be put back together after they have quietly fallen apart.

At the coffee shop, he ordered the Bottomless Cup. The waitress did not make any other suggestions. The price of coffee did not carry any overwhelming need for exchanged remarks.

He looked into the cup and tried to read its dark contents. He set the coffee back down on the table to cool. He wished that there had been a newspaper in the box out front. The Thursday paper sold according to the cents-off food coupons.

The couple at the table next to him had ordered the Barnyard Bonanza Buffet. It was $3.95 and carried the slogan "all-you-care-to-eat."

Nathan found the system in their numerous trips to the food bar. Their first plates were loaded with protein. The man's plate carried an equal number of bacon strips and sausage links, twelve pieces in all. The woman started to select the links, but changed her mind in mid-air, and picked up several sausage patties with a pair of silver tongs. Between their plates, Nathan estimated a scrambled egg count of nine eggs. It was enough to empty any small farmyard of life.

Their next plates were for the carbohydrates: hotcakes, French toast, and biscuits, all covered in cane syrup; grits and butter, and hash-brown potatoes and ketchup. And these were followed closely by the fruits-of-the-season plates laden with orange slices and melon plugs.

As the couple were asking the waitress whether the soup of the day came with the Barnyard Bonanza, Nathan looked outside the window. He was a little embarrassed that he didn't have anything better to do than to see how much food people could eat. It kind of reminded Nathan of something a radio-preacher had said once over the airwaves late at night about fast days. "Yes," he said, "keep them when there's neither bread nor bacon in the cupboard."

In the vacant lot next to the coffee shop, a young man had posted a sign that read *Merry-Go-Round Rides $1.00.* It was not the brightly painted and ornamented apparatus of the circus that played every year beside the state fair. It was reduced to bare bones, to wooden poles without a touch of paint. And the sculpted wooden horses were replaced by one broken nag pulled along by a frayed rope.

Nathan gave up his right to the Bottomless Cup of coffee. He walked over to the lot. He longed for something beautiful.

There was no music. The wood creaked as it turned in a tight circle. With a stick and shouts the young man drove a grey horse. The horse's once smooth coat was sliced by the plain shape of bones.

Nathan watched a boy that seemed far too heavy jumping up, now and again, upon the horse's sloped back. The horse moved stiffly around the ring in an absent-minded way.

Nathan looked at the multiplicity of half-ring shapes that the animal's hoofs had made in the sand.

"Care for a turn?" the young man asked.

Nathan was startled. "That horse," he said, "looks like it's ready for the pasture."

"Just a pure waste of space. It wasn't even worth shooting when I got it."

"It looks like it's starving," Nathan continued.

"It's just *lean*. You know, *a horse is a horse, of course, of course* ...."

Nathan didn't understand the man. He had never watched *Mister Ed* on television. He had never seen any talking-horse shows. But once he had seen a movie about Francis, The Talking Mule, who managed to cause a great deal of trouble for his innocent sidekick, Donald O'Connor. What Nathan did next he understood even less.

"Why not sell it and get a *real* horse?" Nathan asked.

The man swatted the horse's back with the stick. He felt that special feeling of value for an unwanted item that someone else covets.

Nathan offered the man three hundred dollars for the horse. It was a high price, but Nathan had never bought a horse before. In fact, Nathan hadn't bought much of anything in years outside of a few irreclaimable items picked up at garage sales.

Nathan went home and waited in his backyard for the man to deliver the horse. It was a small yard, even by beach house standards. Nathan had never been one to want to putter around in a garden or trim shrubs to look like things other than shrubs.

Inside, the house had dwindled to a single room where his wife sat stacking and restacking magazines. She thought about buying an Early American magazine rack to go beside the couch.

Outside, Nathan imagined her discovering the horse. She would stand beside it. She wouldn't say a word. There comes a point where there's no more virtue in words. Then her hand would brush the fuzzy hairs that radiated about the horse's eyes. She would not know why she did this. She would feel the hot flushing of her face, and strain to say, "Good boy." And without touching, it would be like Nathan and his wife were holding hands.

"It won't be long," thought Nathan, as he waited in the yard.

ALLEN WOODMAN was born in Alabama, in 1954. He was educated at Huntingdon College and Florida State University, where he received a University Fellowship. His short stories have appeared in *Carolina Quarterly*, *Epoch*, *The North American Review*, *The Crescent Review*, and other magazines. His work has been cited in *Best American Short Stories* and in The Pushcart Prize Series. Now living in Flagstaff, Arizona, Allen teaches creative writing at Northern Arizona University, writes, and publishes Word Beat Press.

ROSS ZIRKLE has recently moved to Woodland Park, Colorado. He is a full-time artist there, working mainly in lithographs and pen-and-ink. Ross illustrates all of the fiction for Swallow's Tale Press.